Roles in Movie Making

George Ivanoff

Contents

Movie Making 2

The Process of Making Movies 2

Overall Control 4

Pre-Production 8

Production 14

Post-Production 21

Every Movie Is Different 26

How to Make a Movie 28

Glossary 31

Index 32

Movie Making

The Process of Making Movies

Making a movie is a long and complicated process. It is a **collaborative** effort, involving many people with different skills.

An actor's role in the movie-making process is well known, as actors are the people who play the characters. Actors are the ones who usually become famous. But there are other people with important roles in the movie-making process, from those who write the words that the actors speak to the people who design and make the costumes.

Actors like Viola Davis are famous because people see them on-screen, unlike the people who work behind the camera.

The movie-making process can be broken down into three stages:

- pre-production, which is everything that happens before filming starts
- production, or what happens during filming
- post-production, or what happens after filming is finished.

Only a few people work on a movie all the way through, but many others are involved during the different stages. Their roles cover a wide range of tasks and responsibilities.

Workers set up cameras and lighting for a movie.

Many people doing different jobs work together to create the movies people enjoy in cinemas.

Overall Control

There are some key people who are involved in every stage of the movie-making process. These people have overall responsibility and control over the movie.

Executive Producer

The executive producer is responsible for raising the money that is needed to make the movie.

Sometimes, the executive producer provides the money to fund the movie themselves. But most of the time, they will source the money from a **movie studio**, a **production company** or a **film investment firm**.

The bulk of the executive producer's work is completed before pre-production even starts. From then on, they keep an eye on every stage, making sure things stay within the **budget**, but they are not heavily involved in the movie-making process.

Often, more than one person will fill the role of executive producer.

Executive producers hold many business meetings to source the money for a movie.

Producer

The producer also oversees all the stages of the movie-making process.

A major part of a producer's role is to manage the budget, which means working out how much money is needed to make the movie and what the money will be spent on. The role also involves hiring other people who will work on the movie, such as the director and scriptwriter, and then supervising all those people.

Sometimes, more than one person will fill the role of producer. Although they have a very important role, producers rarely become famous in the way that other people who work on movies can.

Producer Brian Grazer (right) and famous director Ron Howard (left) have made more than 20 movies together.

Director

The director oversees the creative side of the whole movie-making process.

The director's main role is to guide the actors and help them shape their performances as the movie is being filmed. But the director also does much more, from helping the scriptwriter to develop the story to deciding what **scenes** to film and how to film them. The director also helps to make decisions about **editing** and music.

Because the role is so vast, the director will usually have an assistant director, and sometimes even a second assistant director.

Storyboards

Directors will often use storyboards to help plan out the details of each scene that needs to be created. A storyboard is similar to a comic book, with drawings that show all the movement in a scene. Storyboards are particularly useful for planning out action sequences where lots of things are happening at once.

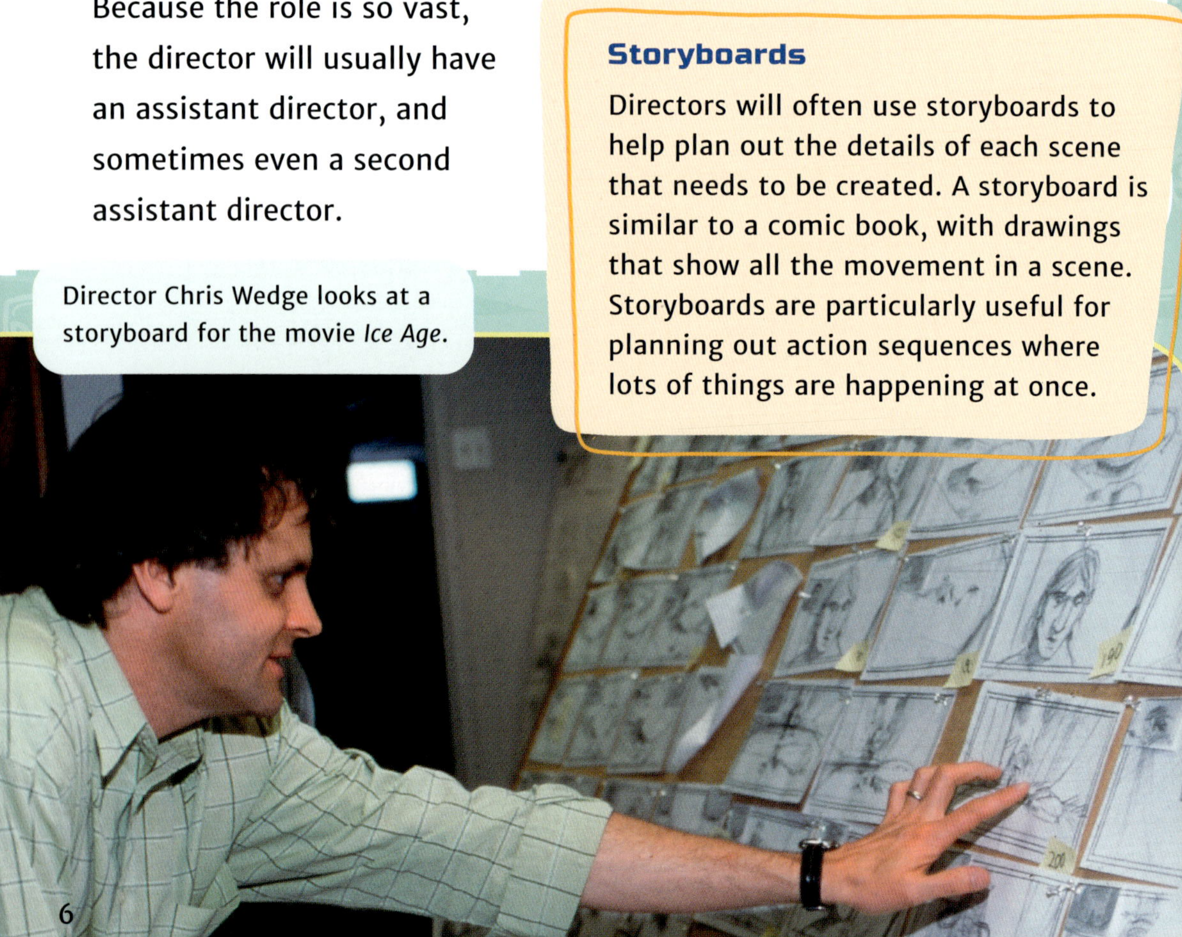

Director Chris Wedge looks at a storyboard for the movie *Ice Age*.

Famous Directors

Some directors are as famous as actors.

- Alfred Hitchcock directed over 50 movies between 1922 and 1976. He is known for appearing in most of his movies, if only briefly and never in a speaking role.
- Steven Spielberg has directed many popular movies, including *E.T. the Extra-Terrestrial*, the first two *Jurassic Park* movies and most of the *Indiana Jones* movies.

Alfred Hitchcock sits next to the camera while directing a movie in the late 1940s.

Steven Spielberg crouches next to a fake dinosaur as he directs *The Lost World: Jurassic Park*.

Pre-Production

Pre-production is the first stage in movie making. This stage includes a range of tasks that need to happen before **shooting** can begin. Pre-production can last many months, and sometimes even years. There are many people whose roles begin in this stage of the process.

Scriptwriter

The scriptwriter writes the script for the movie, also known as the screenplay. The script contains all of the **dialogue** spoken by the actors, as well as the emotions they need to portray and the actions they need to perform. It also describes everything that will appear on the screen, such as the **location** and the action happening around the actors. The scriptwriter might adapt an existing novel or play, or they might create an entirely new story.

Emma Thompson (right) worked as both a scriptwriter and an actor on the movie *Nanny McPhee*, which she starred in along with Angela Lansbury (left).

The scriptwriter will often begin by writing a treatment, which is a summary of the plot and characters, and might include a description of the main scenes. Then, they will turn the treatment into a full script. The director and producers are sometimes involved in writing the script or providing the scriptwriter with feedback.

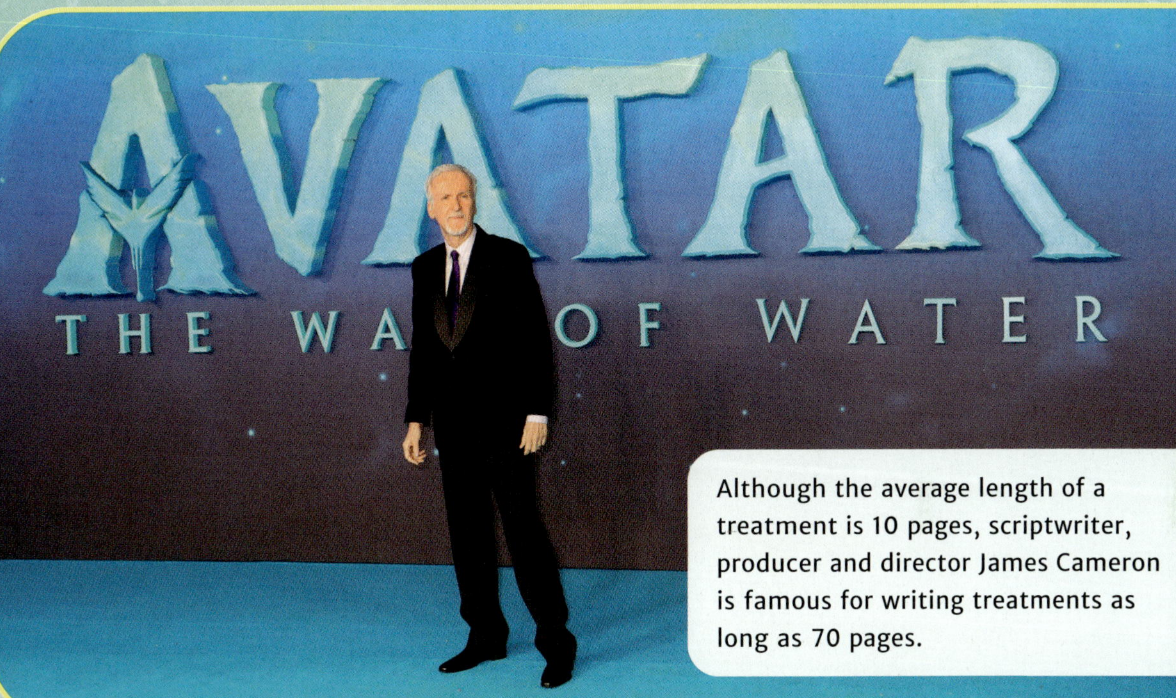

Although the average length of a treatment is 10 pages, scriptwriter, producer and director James Cameron is famous for writing treatments as long as 70 pages.

Writing the Percy Jackson Movies

Although author Rick Riordan wrote the Percy Jackson book *The Sea of Monsters*, a scriptwriter named Marc Guggenheim adapted the novel into a movie. The book had too many details to include in a movie, so Guggenheim decided which parts of the story to focus on and which parts to leave out.

Casting Director

The casting director helps the movie's director to decide which actors should be **cast**. Usually, the casting director will consider lots of actors for each of the different roles, and then create a shortlist for the director to choose from. Sometimes, the casting director will hold **auditions** to find the most suitable actors; other times, they will base the decision on actors' performances in previous movies. The movie director then makes the final choice on which actors to cast in all the important roles.

The casting director starts by casting the major parts, and then works through the list of supporting and minor parts. With minor acting parts, it is the casting director who makes the final decision about who to cast.

Casting directors will hold auditions to find the actor that's most suited to each role.

Production Designer

The production designer is responsible for designing the **sets** and choosing the locations where the movie will be shot.

After the sets have been designed, the production designer will then supervise the building process. When working at specific locations, the production designer will make decisions about adding or removing elements from the sets. For example, shop signs and window displays may be added to a city street so that the location will look the way it needs to for the movie.

Desert Additions

The outdoor scenes on the fictional planet of Tatooine in the movie *Star Wars: Episode IV – A New Hope* were shot in Tunisia, Africa. The moisture farm where Luke Skywalker lived and worked with his aunt and uncle had to be designed and then built in the desert location by the production designer and their **crew**.

Costume Designer

The costume designer decides what clothing all the actors will wear. The costume designer will then buy the clothes that are needed and design any other clothes that need to be made.

This role often requires lots of research, especially for movies set in the past or another country, to make sure the costumes are accurate for the time and place.

The role also requires a great deal of imagination, particularly for science fiction and fantasy movies, when costume designers have to create futuristic clothing or clothes that magical beings would wear.

The costume designer also supervises all the people who work in the costume department, including the people who make the clothes.

Costume designer Jacqueline Durran created accurate old-fashioned clothes for *Little Women*, a movie set in the 1860s.

Video Game Costumes

For the *Sonic the Hedgehog* movie, costume designer Debra McGuire needed to create costumes for actor Jim Carrey to wear as Dr Robotnik. She had to find real clothes based on what the animated character wore in the original video game.

Hair and Make-up Designer

The hair and make-up designer is responsible for the way actors look on-screen. This could be as simple as making the actors look natural. It might also involve creating an accurate historical look – for example, elaborate wigs and white make-up for a movie set in England during the rule of Queen Elizabeth I. Designers might even need to create fantasy make-up for elves or horror make-up for zombies.

Sometimes, the hair and make-up designer will work with a special effects designer. For example, a horror movie might need **prosthetic** limbs that gush blood, or a science fiction movie might need an alien mask with movable antennae.

The hair and make-up designer also supervises all the hairstylists and make-up artists during the production stage of the movie.

Rick Baker, who worked as both a make-up designer and a special effects designer, checks the make-up on one of the actors in *Planet of the Apes*.

Production

Production refers to the second stage of movie making, when the shooting of the movie takes place. At this stage, even more people become involved.

Cinematographer

The cinematographer, also known as the director of photography, is responsible for the way the movie is filmed. This role includes being in charge of the lighting and camerawork.

The cinematographer helps the director decide where to place the camera for each scene and how the camera will move. For example, a scene could have a long sweeping shot of a landscape, or a static (not moving) close-up of an actor's face. The cinematographer will also decide how best to light each scene.

Sometimes, the cinematographer operates the main camera. If not, they will supervise the camera operator, as well as the rest of the camera crew. This includes the gaffer, who is the chief electrician, the grips, who set up and move the cameras, and the focus puller, who adjusts the focus while the camera is in operation.

A cinematographer operates a camera on a moving trolley.

Scenes vs Shots

A scene is often made up of multiple shots. A shot is part of a scene that is filmed without stopping. For example, a scene of two people talking might be made up of three shots – a wide shot of both people, a close-up of one person and then a close-up of the other person.

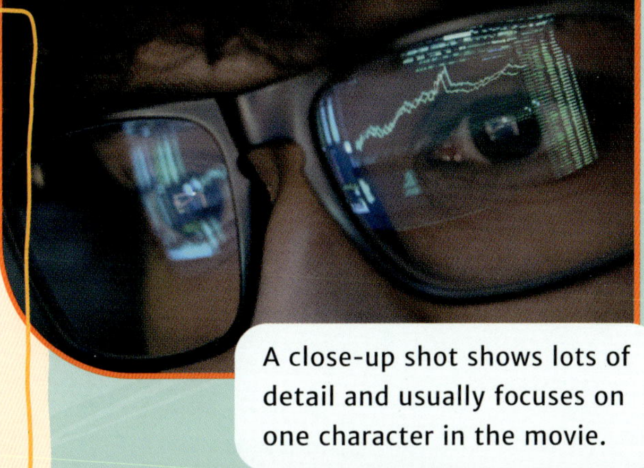

A close-up shot shows lots of detail and usually focuses on one character in the movie.

A wide shot shows more of the scene, often including all of the characters or scenery.

Takes

Each shot that is filmed is called a take. Sometimes, several takes must be filmed because mistakes are made, such as a line spoken incorrectly or a poorly positioned light casting a shadow on an actor's face. A new take can also be filmed if the director thinks of a different way of doing the shot.

Sound Recordist

The sound recordist records all of the sounds made during shooting by using a variety of microphones, depending on the shot. For close-ups, a **boom microphone** might be used so that the microphone isn't visible on-screen. For very wide shots, a **radio microphone** would be used because a boom microphone wouldn't be able to pick up the sounds. Some shots might even require the use of multiple microphones. The sound recordist monitors the sound as it is being recorded to ensure that it is clear and usable.

The sound recordist also supervises other people in the sound crew, such as the boom operator and the sound assistants.

A boom microphone is being used in this scene to capture the sounds made by the actor.

Special Effects Supervisor

The special effects supervisor is responsible for all the special effects that take place on set. This might be as simple as positioning a wind machine to make it look like a windy day. But the role can also include more complicated things, such as setting up explosions or creating bullet holes.

A special effects supervisor can set up large explosions that are often needed for action movies.

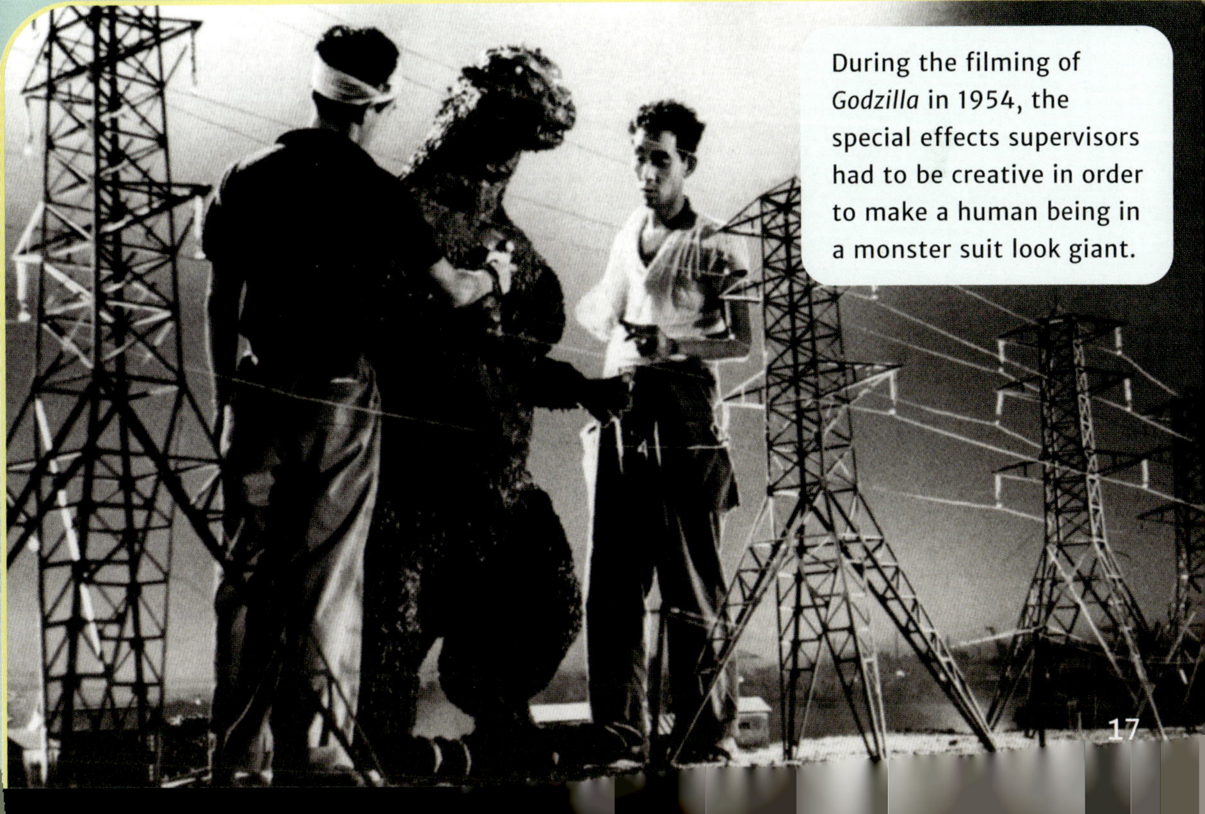

During the filming of *Godzilla* in 1954, the special effects supervisors had to be creative in order to make a human being in a monster suit look giant.

Stunt Coordinator

The stunt coordinator is responsible for organising all the stunts in a movie, including falls, fights and any other piece of action that is too dangerous for the actors to perform.

The stunt coordinator plans every part of how the stunts will be done. For example, a fall from a building would involve planning where to position the **inflatable** landing pads to cushion the stunt performer's fall and what sort of protective gear the stunt performer will need to wear.

An inflatable landing pad is set up below a window that a stunt performer will jump from.

The stunt coordinator supervises the stunt performers to make sure that the stunts are done in a safe way. Sometimes, the actors will perform simpler stunts themselves. In that case, the stunt coordinator provides special training to ensure the actor can perform the action safely.

Stunt coordinator Andreas Petrides (right) practises a lightsaber fight in costume with one of the actors from *Star Wars: Episode I – The Phantom Menace*.

Actor Stunts

Actor Tom Cruise is famous for doing many of his own stunts, including dangerous ones. For example, in the *Mission: Impossible* movies, he leapt from one building to another and even drove a motorcycle off a cliff.

Other Roles

There are many more people who work on a movie during production, from cable pullers, who make sure any electrical cables are secured safely, to the caterers, who feed the actors and crew.

Actors in a movie take a break to eat lunch while still in costume.

There are also people called extras – people who appear in movies but don't have any lines to speak. They often make up a crowd or act as bystanders in the background of a scene.

A large crowd of extras gathers on a set where a scene is about to be filmed.

Post-Production

The post-production stage occurs after shooting is completed. In this stage, all the different elements of the movie are combined. There are many people whose roles begin in this stage of the process.

Film Editor

The film editor views all the takes of the many shots that make up the different scenes. There could be thousands of individual takes!

Once the final takes are chosen, the editor places them into a logical sequence using special computer software. This is time-consuming and detailed work.

Film editors use special software in order to put the entire movie together in the right order.

Film editor Ralph Dietrich used a device that let him see what was on a film strip before he cut it.

Cutting Film

Prior to digital technology, films were edited by hand. A film editor would actually have to cut pieces of film and glue them together in the required order.

Visual Effects Supervisor

The visual effects supervisor is responsible for all the visual effects that are added after shooting has finished. This can include adding computer-generated imagery (CGI), as well as creating and filming models of spaceships, planes or buildings. Science fiction, fantasy and horror movies are known for having realistic or magical visual effects. But there are other types of movies that also need them. For example, a historical movie filmed at an old mansion might need visual effects to remove the modern buildings in the background.

If lots of visual effects are needed for a movie, the visual effects supervisor will be in charge of a large team of people. Sometimes, a visual effects company is hired that specialises in particular effects, such as editing shots to remove wires that are attached to an actor in a flying sequence of a superhero movie.

A visual effects supervisor could create a background and turn an actor into a monster for this scene, in post-production.

Sound Designer

The sound designer chooses the sound effects that will be added to the movie. This includes realistic sounds that viewers are familiar with, as well as unfamiliar sounds. For example, after the visual effect of a huge meteor striking Earth has been added in a science fiction movie, the sound designer would create the sounds that they think the crash would make.

If a movie scene is set in a large empty cave, but has really been shot on a set, the sound designer might add an echo to the actors' voices to make the scene more realistic.

Sound designers record chains rattling and a drill buzzing in order to add sounds to a scene with a robot.

Composer

The composer writes the music that is heard throughout the movie. This music is called a musical score, or simply a score.

The score is used to emphasise the mood of particular scenes. The composer will work closely with the director to decide on the mood and style of the music for each scene.

Often, the composer will also conduct the orchestra that plays the score, but sometimes there is a separate conductor.

John Williams conducts an orchestra that is playing a musical score for an audience.

Famous Themes

Movie composers can become famous for their well-known movie scores. John Williams is famous for creating the music for movies such as the *Star Wars* saga, the *Indiana Jones* movies and the first two *Jurassic Park* movies. Michael Giacchino built on Williams's work with scores for *Jurassic World* and *Rogue One: A Star Wars Story*. He also combined many musical themes from other superhero movies in *Spider-Man: No Way Home*.

Michael Giacchino (right) reviews a score with another composer in a studio.

Music Supervisor

The music supervisor organises any additional music that's used in the movie. Sometimes, movies use famous songs or existing pieces of music. For example, a pop song could be used during the opening titles or closing credits. Other movies might make use of classical music at key moments. The music supervisor is the person who organises these pieces of music. They might need to obtain permission to use an existing song or piece of music, or they might hire a singer and musicians to record a particular song.

The *Fantasia* movies combine animation with pieces of classical music.

Every Movie Is Different

The number of people who work on a movie really depends on the movie itself. A lot depends on money!

A big-budget Hollywood blockbuster might have hundreds of people working on it – not only creative people, but also accountants, animal trainers and truck drivers. However, a small independent movie could be made with just a dozen people.

A Big Budget

Costing over US$280 million to make, *The Lord of the Rings* movie trilogy employed over 2400 production staff and 26000 extras.

A large group of production staff works together on a scene in *The Lord of the Rings: The Two Towers*.

The way in which movies are made has changed over time, and so have the roles of the people involved. For many years, movies were silent, so there wasn't a need for sound recordists or sound designers. And for an even longer time, movies were shot in black and white. CGI wasn't widely used in movies until the 1980s.

There is so much to explore in the world of movie making!

There are many different roles in the movie-making process that are interesting to learn about.

How to Make a Movie

Making a movie for fun or as part of a school project can be a great way to learn about the movie-making process. There is a lot of technology that is readily available to help you. A whole movie can be made using a tablet or a smartphone!

Apps

There are many different tablet and smartphone **apps** that could help with your movie making. There are video editing apps for putting the scenes together, music apps to help you create your own score, and even apps to create visual effects.

Goal

To make a short movie, using the three stages of the movie-making process

Materials

Essential:

- a tablet or smartphone with a camera

Optional:

- apps for editing, adding music, etc.

- props to use in the video

The More the Merrier

Get a group of people together and decide on who will fill each role in the movie-making process. It's okay for one person to fill more than one role. You won't have to fill all the roles that have been described in this book. In fact, you could do it all by yourself if you wanted!

Steps

Pre-Production

1. Write a script. Keep it short and simple.
2. Decide where you will shoot the movie and what you'll need, for example, actors, props and costumes.
3. Discuss who will act in your movie. You might not even need actors – you could make a movie about your pets!
4. Prepare your equipment. Use a tablet or a smartphone to film your movie. Make sure you have any apps you want to use.
5. Plan a shooting schedule. Include details such as locations and which scenes will be filmed where and in what order. Will you shoot the scenes out of order, and then edit them together later? Or will you shoot the whole movie in order?

Production

1. Set up your first scene. Decide where the actors will go and where the camera will be.
2. Rehearse the scene.
3. Shoot the scene.
4. Repeat for each of the remaining scenes.

Post-Production

1. If the scenes were shot out of order, edit them together using an editing app on your device so that they're in a logical sequence. If the scenes were shot in order, decide whether you want to edit by shortening some scenes, or maybe even removing some.
2. Add any visual effects or text.
3. Decide if you need to add any sound effects. Most video editing apps will have a range of sound effects that you can use.
4. Choose a song or some music to add. You could even create your own piece of music.
5. Show the movie to your family and friends.

Glossary

apps (*noun*) applications, or programs, that are downloaded to a mobile device

auditions (*noun*) test performances done by actors who want to be in a movie

boom microphone (*noun*) a microphone that is attached to a special pole called a boom

budget (*noun*) an amount of money that can be spent

cast (*verb*) chosen to act in a movie

collaborative (*adjective*) done by two or more people working together

crew (*noun*) people working on a movie who are not actors

dialogue (*noun*) words spoken by characters in a movie

editing (*noun*) the process of piecing together shots and scenes to make a complete movie

film investment firm (*noun*) a company that supplies money for making movies

inflatable (*adjective*) able to reach its full size by being filled with air

location (*noun*) a place where a movie scene is filmed

movie studio (*noun*) a large company that makes, owns and distributes movies

production company (*noun*) a company that only makes movies

prosthetic (*adjective*) human-made as a replacement or fake part of the body, such as an arm or a leg

radio microphone (*noun*) a microphone that isn't connected to a wire

scenes (*noun*) parts of a movie that happen in a particular place at a particular time

sets (*noun*) the scenery that is put together as settings for a movie

shooting (*noun*) the filming of a movie

Index

actor 2, 6, 7, 8, 10, 12, 13, 14, 15, 16, 18, 19, 20, 22, 23, 29, 31
apps 28, 29, 30, 31
auditions 10, 31
Baker, Rick 13
boom microphone 16, 31
budget 4, 5, 26, 31
casting director 10
cinematographer 14
composer 24
computer-generated imagery (CGI) 22, 27
costume designer 12
crew 11, 14, 16, 20, 31
Cruise, Tom 19
dialogue 8, 31
director 5, 6–7, 9, 10, 14, 15, 24
editing 6, 21, 22, 28, 29, 30, 31
executive producer 4
film editor 21
film investment firm 4, 31
Giacchino, Michael 24
Guggenheim, Marc 9
hair and make-up designer 13
Hitchcock, Alfred 7
locations 8, 11, 29, 31
McGuire, Debra 12
movie studio 4, 31
music supervisor 25
producer 5, 9
production company 4, 31
production designer 11
radio microphone 16, 32
scenes 6, 9, 11, 14, 15, 16, 20, 21, 22, 23, 24, 26, 28, 29, 30, 31, 32
scriptwriter 5, 6, 8–9
sets 11, 12, 13, 17, 20, 23, 32
shooting 8, 14, 16, 21, 22, 29, 32
shots 14–15, 16, 21, 22, 31
sound designer 23, 27
sound recordist 16, 27
special effects supervisor 17
Spielberg, Steven 7
storyboard 6
stunt coordinator 18–19
stunt performer 18–19
takes 15, 21
visual effects supervisor 22
Williams, John 24